Sammy Squirrel & Rodney Raccoon
A STANLEY PARK TALE

by Duane Lawrence
illustrations by Gordon Clover

SAMMY SQUIRREL & RODNEY RACCOON

A STANLEY PARK TALE

by Duane Lawrence

illustrations by Gordon Clover

Library and Archives Canada Cataloguing in Publication

Lawrence, Duane, 1956-
    Sammy Squirrel & Rodney Raccoon : a Stanley Park tale / by Duane Lawrence ; illustrated by Gordon Clover.

ISBN 978-1-894694-54-4

    1. Human-animal relationships--Juvenile fiction. I. Clover, Gordon II. Title. III. Title: Sammy Squirrel and Rodney Raccoon.
PS8573.A904S23 2007   jC813'.6   C2007-904353-4

First Printing October 2007
Printed in Canada

Granville Island
Publishing

Suite 212–1656 Duranleau
Vancouver, BC, Canada V6H 3S4
Tel 604-688-0320 Toll-free 1-877-688-0320
www.granvilleislandpublishing.com

Illustrations by Gordon Clover

Book design and layout by Momentum Productions
www.momentumproductions.net

for Joey

Contents

1

The Surprisingly Dangerous Nut Haul

Sammy Squirrel awoke to the sound of a long, deep howl and leapt out of bed. Rushing to the window, he looked out to see what had made such a terrible noise. The large branches of his giant fir tree swooshed and swayed in every direction. It was the wind—a clear sign that winter would soon arrive in Stanley Park.

Oh dear, he muttered to himself, *I'd better finish my nut gathering before any snow falls.* He'd always felt this was a wonderful way to spend a late autumn day. But on this morning it was raining "people and pets," as the old animal expression goes. And that would make going on a nut haul an unpleasant task for any squirrel, even a good-natured, hardworking one like Sammy.

After a delicious breakfast of roasted acorns and green leaf tea, Sammy hurriedly dressed in his green rain hat and coat, grabbed his favourite green umbrella, and scurried toward the door. He stopped for a moment to admire himself in the hallway mirror.

Oh, I love green things! Evergreen, forest green, anything green! And I do look good in green, too—somewhat like a little green shrub, come to think of it.

Full of admiration for the stylish reflection he had seen in the mirror, Sammy opened the door and peered out. Wriggling his nose, he sniffed the air as a quick safety check, for an unfriendly hawk might be lurking in the treetops at this time of day. Satisfied there was no sign of danger from the animal world, he hurried down the tree and headed along the winding trail in his fancy "green shrub" attire.

He paused before crossing a path, because people and pets could show up unexpectedly almost anywhere these days. He'd heard stories about them suddenly dashing around with a great commotion that scared the wits out of everyone.

Very rude and dangerous behaviour, he thought.

There was a time when most people and pets would only visit the outskirts of this enormous park by the Great Ocean. The sounds of their comings and goings along the seawall path had been a distant murmur that existed in a very different world. But that had all changed. Now a multitude of people and pets frequently veered off the usual path to explore the natural world— posing a new danger that every animal in the park had to be aware of.

Stopping in front of a gigantic fir tree near the entrance to Beaver Lake Trail, Sammy tried to remember where he had buried his last nut haul.

Was it right here at the base of the tree or up between those two large roots over there? he muttered to himself, not wishing to attract any attention, and certainly not wanting anyone to see him in this predicament. After all, a squirrel unable to find his nut haul—what would the other animals say? Surely they would laugh uproariously.

Think, squirrel, think, he murmured to himself. *Ah, it must be at the fork between the large tree roots.*

Now that the rain had stopped, he put down his green umbrella and took out his small shovel. Gripping it in his left paw (for he was a left-pawed squirrel and proud of it), he began digging…and digging, and digging, and digging…a little to the left, a little to the right, then a little more toward the tree, then a little more away from the tree. Nothing. No nut haul.

Staring at the ground before him, he mumbled to himself, *left…no…right…no…up there… no…back here….* Sammy didn't notice the small group of animals who had, one by one, gathered a short distance away from him to watch. Squirty Skunk was the first to speak.

"Good morning, Sammy Squirrel," he said in a rather loud voice. Startled, Sammy jumped in the air, dropped his shovel and landed flat on his bottom. All the animals laughed at the sight.

"Well, you might have let me know you were there with a little more animal-like civility," Sammy replied abruptly, looking away from the other animals while he regained his composure and brushed off his lovely green raincoat.

"Yes, I suppose we could have, but you seemed to be searching for something so desperately that

13

we were all caught up in the drama of it," replied Dolores Duck, who had waddled over from the lake in response to the strange sounds coming from what looked like a green shrub hopping around the base of a big fir tree. Knowing full well that shrubs are not the hopping type, due to their firmly planted roots, Dolores had become extremely curious.

"It is rude to just stand and gawk," said Dolores, "but discovering it was you in such a frenzy, why, I was just quackless!"

"I thought you were some strange shrub from a distance, too," said Benjamin Beaver. "Like Dolores, I was quite overcome at the sight of a leaping little green bush and simply had to investigate. Then to find you, Sammy Squirrel, digging so furiously—well!"

"Yes, furiously, furiously, furiously!" squeaked the field mice in unison.

"What in the world were you hopping around for?" enquired Renée Rabbit. "You looked like a small green rabbit for a moment, but I knew you couldn't be a rabbit, because rabbits can be many colours but never green," she laughed.

Sammy Squirrel was not laughing, however. If

anything, he was somewhat embarrassed. "Well, if you must know, I'm on a nut haul. In case you haven't noticed, winter will be here soon, and I for one plan to be prepared for it," he stated confidently. Raising his head high, he planted the tip of his shovel in the ground and coolly looked around at the small group of animals in front of him.

Before any of the animals could say another word, they heard a furious fluttering of wings from high above them. Penelope Pigeon, an unusual sight in this part of the park, swooped overhead and yelled down, "People and pets, people and pets! Quickly, everyone, run to your homes!"

At the very mention of the first "P" word, all the animals went into a terrible panic. Dolores and Benjamin turned and ran to the lake; Squirty scurried into the woods; Renée jumped into the dense grass; and the field mice scattered in all directions. Everyone ran as fast as they could.

Sammy started to scamper up the trunk of the enormous fir tree. But in his rush to escape, he left his pocket shovel on the ground.

"Oh no," he cried out. "I've left my shovel!"

Down the tree he scrambled. He grabbed it, but by this time two very large shadows had invaded the animal world. It was too late for Sammy to scurry back up the tree. Running toward Beaver Lake was useless because he didn't know how to swim, and running toward the woods would only attract attention. So he turned his back to the shadows and stood very still, although he couldn't stop trembling with fear.

Now he could clearly see the large shadows that passed nearby—one tall and thin, the other low and long. They moved very quickly, perhaps running, which seemed to be the custom of these large creatures.

Oh, if only I could stop shaking, he thought, *then they wouldn't notice me.* But no matter how hard he tried, he kept on quivering. The large shadow appeared to move away, while the smaller one turned in his direction, slowed down and sniffed the air. Suddenly, it started to growl right in the direction of Sammy Squirrel!

"What is it, Duke?" a booming voice said. "Come on, now, let's finish our run. There's nothing there. It's only the wind rustling the small bushes and trees. You're imagining things."

I'm a rustling bush, a rustling bush, a rustling bush, Sammy frantically repeated to himself over and over.

And a rustling bush he did appear to be! With one sharp tug from the larger shadow and a yelp from the smaller one, the two were off down the trail as quickly as they had come.

Sammy, however, didn't move. For the longest time he was glued to the spot, his whole body shaking. Finally, when the trembling stopped, he turned his head slowly toward the trail. He could still see the two fast-moving figures across the lake. They disappeared down the wide trail that led to the outskirts of the park near the Great Ocean. Sammy was safe.

Dolores Duck appeared at the edge of Beaver Lake but didn't dare step out of the water. "Sammy, Sammy, are you all right?" she asked in a high-pitched quack.

"I…I…yes, I…I think so," he faintly replied.

"Oh, Sammy, did you hear them? They thought you were a little green shrub, like we did! Oh, how lucky you are!"

Yes, the green rain hat and green raincoat had done it, he thought. Green was more than just his favourite colour, green had a different meaning for him now. He was alive. Green had saved him. No, greenery had saved him! The trees, the bushes, the shrubs, the grass, Sammy felt grateful to them all.

How odd, he thought, *I owe my life to them. I owe my life to greenery.*

"Go home now and rest, Sammy," Dolores said. "You've had an awful scare. Finish your nut gathering another day." Sammy nodded weakly, turned away and walked down the winding trail back to his tree, deep in the heart of the woods. Now and again he looked around and exclaimed to no one in particular, "Greenery, greenery, oh, thank you, dear greenery!"

2

Rodney Raccoon and the Marshmallow Matter

Rodney Raccoon, Sammy's dearest friend, was blissfully unaware of Sammy's close encounter with people and pets. Rodney had spent the morning on the far side of Stanley Park near Lost Lagoon, where he had discovered an easy way to get his breakfast. Someone had been leaving soft, sweet marshmallows under the arched bridge by the stream that led out of the lagoon. And oh, how delicious they were! No work was involved at all, because the little marshmallows were shiny white and clean and didn't need to be washed. This pleased Rodney immensely, since washing food was always such a chore when he was hungry.

But Rodney wasn't the only one to have found

this wonderful cache. Several squirrels, two Canada geese, various little birds, and a rather unfriendly skunk were also nibbling away. As there were enough marshmallows for everyone, no one quarreled over the food, and each animal gave the others enough space to dine in a civilized manner. Everyone, that is, except for the skunk, who occasionally glared greedily at the others' food; everyone had to keep an eye on him while they ate their breakfast.

Having filled his belly and now quite content, Rodney ambled off to pay a visit to his dear friend, Sammy. The long walk would be his morning exercise, a perfect end to this wonderful brunch under the bridge at Lost Lagoon.

It was a rainy morning and windy, too, but Rodney didn't mind at all. His thick fur kept him warm in cold weather, and his rain jacket kept him dry. The only thing he worried about was the path leading away from the arched bridge at the lagoon. People and pets were there in large numbers today, so Rodney knew he had to be on guard. He moved quickly down the paved path and entered the very first animal trail he saw. Feeling safer now, he slowed his pace and breathed in the fresh park air. He thought, *I am so lucky to live here.*

But after a short distance, Rodney felt a fluttering in his tummy. *That's an odd sensation,* he pondered. *Maybe I haven't had quite enough to eat.*

Then he caught sight of a wild huckleberry bush with its fresh fruits dangling over the trail. "Just a few to complete my breakfast," he said, grabbing large bunches of berries and greedily gobbling them down. "No need even to wash them since the rain has left them shiny and clean."

But as he ambled along, Rodney's belly started to make small rumbling sounds. *Oh dear, maybe the huckleberries were too tart?* he thought. *I just might need something sweet to balance them out.* And spotting a wild blackberry bush up ahead, he decided the sensible thing would be to eat a few of those now. *That'll clear up any bellyache that might be coming on. Yes, just a few,* he thought. So he reached out, took a very large pawful and munched and slurped the berries down. "There, much better," he said, taking another large pawful and gobbling those, too.

Now as he ambled along, however, his tummy felt heavier and heavier, and his pace slowed even more.

"I knew it, I knew it," he said. "I should have washed those marshmallows before I ate them. The huckleberries and the blackberries, too. Any self-respecting raccoon would have done that. The food wasn't cleaned properly, and now I have a bellyache. How could I have been so foolish..." Aching terribly, he crawled down the trail until he saw, at last, his friend's tree house up above.

"Sammy, oh, Sammy, help me, please!" he shouted. "Throw down the rope ladder and let me come up. I've done a very silly thing and you must help me."

But having just made a cup of soothing green leaf tea to calm his rattled nerves, Sammy was in no mood for company. However, it was the voice of his dearest friend, who did, indeed, sound distressed. So Sammy put down his cup, opened the door, and tossed down the rope ladder for guests who were not adept tree climbers. Moaning, whining, wincing, and groaning, Rodney made his way slowly up the ladder to his friend's home.

"Whatever is the matter with you?" Sammy enquired, as he ushered him into the house toward a large comfy armchair by the hearth.

"Well, I spotted some marshmallows, you see, that had been left under the bridge at Lost Lagoon and, thinking they were clean, decided to eat them without even washing them," he explained.

"Are you sure it was the marshmallows?" Sammy asked.

"Oh, yes, I'm sure," Rodney said. "And then I ate huckleberries, and after that, some blackberries, and didn't wash any of them, like any self-respecting raccoon would do, so now I have this terrible bellyache."

Sammy examined his friend and started to laugh. "Why, your belly is as big as a bag of acorns! You've simply eaten too much, too fast. Too many marshmallows, too many huckleberries and too many blackberries, you ravenous raccoon. Too much and too fast!" So Sammy went to the stove and poured Rodney a hot cup of green leaf tea and brought it to him. "Here, sip a little bit of this and rest. You'll feel better soon," Sammy said in a soothing voice. And as usual, Sammy was right. Rodney took two small sips of the tea and fell into a deep sleep in front of the warm fire, safe in the care of his trusted friend.

After a short nap, Rodney awoke, feeling like his old self. But before he could say a word of thanks, Sammy was chattering away at him.

"So you think you've had a bad day? You'll never believe what happened to me. I was on a nut haul this morning, and I was almost devoured by…well, those big…oh…even to mention the words…"

"Bears?" said Rodney, who was very curious but quite unclear as to what had caused such terror in his friend. "Bears or coyotes? Foxes? Hawks from above? An eagle?" he queried rapidly, trying to coax the words from his little friend.

"Oh no, much more frightening than any of those!"

But Rodney could not imagine anything more frightening than almost being devoured by bears.

"Well, what were they, for goodness sake?" Rodney asked impatiently.

"People and pets," Sammy whispered, as if saying the words any louder might cause them to appear in his tree house at that very moment.

"Ah, people and pets, was it?"

"Yes, indeed, it was people and pets; and if I hadn't been wearing my green raingear, I would not be here right now serving you tea and talking to you. They almost attacked me near Beaver Lake, then reconsidered because they thought I was a little green shrub rustling in the wind. Greenery saved me, do you see? Oh, how lucky we are to live in a large and beautiful green park to protect us," he said in one long stretch without stopping for a breath.

"Yes, I see. Well, I suppose you certainly have been a lucky squirrel," Rodney replied calmly, his eyes still on the fire.

"I was almost devoured!" Sammy cried. "Is that boring to you?"

"Oh, no, dear friend, no. I'm most concerned for you and so glad to see you well and safe. It's just that…" Rodney paused for a moment. "Do you think you were really in so much danger?"

Sammy, as the saying goes, lost his nut over that remark. "What do you mean? Of course I was! People and pets are dangerous. You've heard stories from other animals. People and pets are not to be trusted," he sputtered indignantly.

"Well, I suppose some are dangerous and some aren't, just like some of the animals in the park. Some can be trusted and some can't. I think it's quite likely the same with people and pets."

"Well, I for one do not plan to find out!" And suddenly feeling cold, Sammy went to the fire to add a few new twigs.

"I'm feeling so much better now that the sun is out," said Rodney, glancing out the window. "Why don't we take a walk?"

"Well, as long as we stay off Beaver Lake Trail," replied Sammy. "I'm in no mood for any more strange encounters."

No longer in need of their raincoats, they put on warm, autumn sweaters coloured in green and brown weave for camouflage, went out the door, down the rope ladder, and started walking toward Prospect Point in exactly the opposite direction of Beaver Lake.

3

Lord Stanley—Friend or Foe?

Sammy and Rodney ambled along the well-worn path in silence, admiring the gargantuan fir and mighty oak trees. They stopped to sniff wild flowers and marvelled at the greenery with its infinite variety, and myriad shades and hues.

"You know, I think it's true that people and pets aren't all the same," Rodney said, resuming their earlier conversation. "I've heard from a few of the older animals that Lord Stanley, the namesake of our park, was known for his kindness to the animals here."

"Hmmph!" said Sammy indignantly. "Silly rumours, no doubt. But after today's experience it is clear that people and pets are not to be trusted. And I don't want to hear any more about it, Rodney."

The two friends continued their walk in an awkward silence until they came to a soaring cedar tree.

"Look at that sign up there," Rodney said, pointing at the fine, gothic-style lettering. "It says *Judith Raven's Residence*, but I'd swear this is the very same tree where Judy Crow lives."

"You're absolutely right," Sammy chuckled. "She certainly has become pretentious. I've heard she insists that everyone call her Judith now."

"She probably thinks it sounds more elegant."

"I suppose it does, and I'll have to make a special effort not to call her plain old Judy."

"Yes, you'd better. Everyone says she has quite a temper."

Presently, they arrived in front of Old Hollow Hall, where a large meeting was taking place in the trunk of a Douglas fir tree.

"FREE LECTURE" read the notice on the board above the entrance. "Come one, come all. Orlando Owl lectures on the origins of our dear Stanley Park. Not to be missed."

"That sounds interesting!" said Rodney. "And we could ask Orlando if Lord Stanley was kind to animals. Shall we attend?"

Sammy frowned. He was skeptical about anything that dull old owl had to say. But seeing that his friend was excited, he agreed. So they joined the animals—big and small, furry and feathered—pouring into Old Hollow Hall. And on the podium at the front stood Orlando Owl, whose large, intelligent eyes peered confidently at the expectant crowd as they took their seats.

"Who," he said commandingly. "Who," he repeated with dramatic flair. "Who, who, who... was the founder of this great park of ours?"

"Why, Lord Stanley, wasn't it?" two tiny chipmunks chirped, raising their paws simultaneously.

"That is correct, my friends. Lord Stanley it was, and of all the people and pets in the park, Lord Stanley was—you may be shocked to hear—our dearest and kindest friend." He paused as several animals muttered among themselves, astounded by this outrageous news. "Yes—our dearest and kindest friend," he said, repeating the words again as the eyes of every animal gazed up at him. "I was told this by an old raven who had heard that Lord Stanley had ordered the creation of a park for the use and enjoyment of animals of all colours, creeds and customs for all time."

Every animal in the hall gasped!

"Preposterous!" someone shouted out.

"*C'est ridicule!*" said another in a strong
French accent. It was Pierre Beaverre, Benjamin
Beaver's cousin, who was visiting from Quebec.

"Say what? Say really cool?" whispered Rodney
to Sammy.

"He said 'c'est ridicule.' I think it means
'preposterous' in French. Anyway, be quiet! I can't
hear what's going on."

"But I don't know what preposterous means
either!" Rodney whined.

"What Orlando Owl has told you is true," said
a loud voice from the back of the room, "and the
one who told him was my grandfather." All eyes
turned to see Judy Crow, standing proudly at the
entrance to the hall with her feathery coat shined
and oiled.

"You've heard it from Judy," Orlando said.

"That's Judith!" she corrected him.

"I beg your pardon...*Judith*," Orlando bowed.
"And you can ask any of the older animals here
and they will tell you the same thing. There are
many people and pets who are our friends!"

Everyone began muttering again, and the hall was filled with chatter.

"That's it! I've heard enough!" said Sammy, jumping up and hurrying toward the exit.

"Wait!" Rodney said, scurrying after his friend.

"This is preposterous!" Sammy said. "And preposterous means ridiculous, silly, laughable, and outlandish!"

"But what if it's true?"

"You want to put it to a test?" asked Sammy, stopping to look directly at his friend.

"Well, no...maybe...no...yes!" replied Rodney.

"Then let's go on an adventure," Sammy suggested, his eyes now large and bright.

Rodney stopped dead in his tracks. "Are you saying that we...that you and I..."

"Yes, I am. We'll leave tomorrow..."

"Leave Stanley Park? Oh no, oh my goodness!"

"But how else can we know for sure what people and pets are like in this world? We *must* find out for ourselves. Come on, it will be a splendid adventure!"

The two friends looked at each other. Suddenly, Rodney reached out, took both of Sammy's paws and began jumping up and down.

"An adventure, yes, let's do it!" he cried.

And now Sammy started jumping up and down, too. The two dear friends danced around and around!

"An adventure!" they both shouted. "Hooray!"

4

Beyond the Outskirts

The following day was a very busy one for Sammy Squirrel and Rodney Raccoon. First, they made a list of things to take: hats, warm sweaters, raingear, green leaf teabags and a teapot, acorn snacks for Sammy, clams for Rodney, and other odds and ends that any thinking animal would take on a grand adventure beyond the confines of Stanley Park. They gathered all the items and put them in their backpacks in preparation for their departure.

"Done," said Sammy.

"Done," echoed Rodney. They went to bed early that night, so that they would be fully rested for the great journey awaiting them.

The following morning they set off along the winding animal trail that led to the outskirts of the park, facing the Great Ocean. They planned to follow the hidden zigzag path down to the English Bay seawall. If they could get that far without any trouble from people or pets, they would then determine the best route to enter the city of Vancouver.

It was a lovely morning, and the walk was quite agreeable. They talked of what Vancouver might be like, neither one knowing what they might find. And after they had walked for a very long time, Sammy caught a glimpse of the most radiant blue he had ever seen between the giant fir and cedar trees.

"Rodney, do you see that wonderful bluish hue?"

"No, I don't, Sammy. Do you see any wild blueberries for us to munch?"

"Is feeding that belly of yours all you ever think of?" Sammy rolled his eyes.

Stung by his dearest friend's rebuke, Rodney became silent. Then, regaining his pride, he quickly replied, "Well, food is energy and energy is what we'll need for this adventure."

Suddenly, Rodney did glimpse the radiant blue through the trees, and it wasn't like the grey ocean he had seen years ago on a walk one cloudy day. This ocean was very different now that the sky was clear. It was a brilliant blue that sparkled and shone like nothing he had ever seen.

"I see it!" he shouted. "The Great Ocean, I can see it ahead!"

Presently, they came to the edge of a cliff that overlooked the vast expanse of the sparkling Great Ocean. They were at a loss for words. Then, turning their gaze toward the seawall path, they noticed large numbers of people and pets moving in both directions at incredible speeds. It was the busiest commotion they had ever seen.

Sammy led the way down the zigzag path to the seawall and stopped behind a large wall of wild huckleberries at the bottom. Directly ahead, through a small natural arbour, lay the sandy beach and the sparkling ocean framed like a picture.

"Wouldn't it be wonderful to go to the water's edge and touch the sea?" sighed Rodney. "Just for a moment, I mean, before we head down the trail to Vancouver?"

"Wonderfully *dangerous!*" replied Sammy.

"We can run down, stick our paws in, run

back, and be on our way."

Sammy looked out at the sea. It was so large and so beautiful. He longed to feel the water with his paws, too. They looked at each other.

"Yes," said the one.

"Yes," said the other.

And with a count of "one, two, three," off they ran out of the bushes, across the seawall path and onto the beach. Running on the sand was invigorating! It squished between their toes in a marvellous fashion, and the two friends giggled as it tickled their feet. It was a new experience and it was thrilling!

Just then, Rodney heard a sound from behind. It was an odd sound, like a snarling wind—but on this particular day there was only a light breeze.

Turning his head to see what it was, he was suddenly gripped with fear. His worst nightmare had come true! A large number of people and pets were heading directly toward the two friends at lightning speed, and the snarling sound was coming from a very large, vicious-looking dog. The dog's eyes were scrunched tight and his teeth were bared.

"People and pets!" shouted Rodney.

"Quick, run toward the sea!" Sammy hollered back. "It's our only chance!" And both animals ran as fast as they could straight toward the Great Ocean. But just before they reached the water, Sammy spotted a wooden boat on the shoreline. It was Benjamin Beaver's little log boat! "Over there," he cried. "Head for Benjamin's boat!"

Sammy took a gigantic leap, the kind that a very frightened squirrel can make only under the most dire circumstances, and, after flying through the air, landed directly on the seat of the rowboat in front of him.

Seconds later Rodney also reached the boat. Knowing he had no other choice, he shoved the bow with all the raccoon power he could muster. It moved a bit but not enough, so he shoved it again with all his might, and suddenly the boat was free from the shore. Now, Rodney jumped higher than he ever had before and landed squarely in front of a very shocked squirrel. Without a second's delay, he reached for an oar. Sammy grabbed the other one, and they began to row. And they rowed…and rowed…and rowed… for what seemed like an eternity. The two best friends rowed until the large gathering of people

and pets on the shore became tiny specks
behind them.

"Well...now look what you've done," said
Sammy angrily. "How will we ever get to the city?"

"I wasn't the only one who wanted to put a
paw in the sea," Rodney replied. He looked away
from his friend's accusing eyes.

Their arms and legs aching from the whole ordeal, they rowed on in an angry silence.

At last feeling safe from harm, they stopped rowing. Then Rodney Raccoon, head bowed, turned and looked meekly at his best friend.

"I'm sorry, Sammy, you're right," he said. "This is all my fault. Can you ever forgive me?"

Sammy looked back into his friend's sad eyes and sighed. "We both counted 'one, two, three' and ran. If there is fault, we're both to blame. I'm sorry for my outburst, Rodney."

That said, and friends again, they began to discuss the predicament they were in. There was only one thing to do. They would wait until dark and row back to shore when all the people and pets had left Stanley Park. They both agreed that was their safest bet. And so, exhausted from such a close call and weary from rowing, the two friends closed their eyes, leaned against each other and fell fast asleep.

5

Across the Great Ocean

Hours later, Sammy awoke. He looked to the left, then to the right, and slowly turned around to look behind.

Oh my gosh, he thought. *No beach, no beautiful green park, no people, no pets, nothing but the Great Ocean in every direction…wave after wave after wave reaching into the distance and not a cedar or a fir or a maple tree in sight.*

"Wake up, Rodney," Sammy nudged his sleeping friend. "I have some really bad news!"

Rodney slowly opened his eyes and blinked a few times, not quite sure where he was. Collecting his senses, he looked out to where he thought the park was, then around him in the same way his friend had done.

"Oh m-my…oh m-m-my…" he sputtered. "We

are…"

"Lost…at…sea!" Sammy finished the sentence for him, pausing after each word in a most discouraging tone.

Hours passed like an eternity, which they both knew to be a very, very, very long time. The ocean appeared vast and unending, and the sun was beating down on them. Feeling parched, Sammy stretched his arm over the side and cupped a pawful of seawater.

"Phew!" he grimaced and spat the water back. "It tastes like salty soup!"

"Of course it's salty, Sammy, it's seawater. We can't drink it, you silly thing!"

And this made them even more worried. They still had some food in their packs, but they hadn't brought any fresh water with them. More hours passed in a very uncomfortable silence.

"Do you feel a bit small and helpless?" Rodney asked Sammy at last.

"We *are* small and, right now, very helpless," replied Sammy.

Then, in the distance, a tiny black dot appeared on the horizon. It seemed to be moving in their direction, got larger and changed colour from black to gray… then lightened even more, its shape changing again as it drew closer. It grew bigger still and began to look somewhat familiar. Now they could make out a fluttering motion. It had wings. It was white. It was a bird!

"A seagull!" cried Rodney, "We're saved, we're saved!"

It was a seagull indeed, and having flown thousands of miles (and even more in kilometres), this bird was as tired as it was curious at the sight of the little boat on the Great Ocean. The gull swooped down and hovered overhead with the hope that the boat might offer something in the way of food or refuge. But to his great surprise the seagull found a raccoon and a squirrel in the middle of the ocean.

"Ahoy, mateys," said the seagull, landing on the bow of the boat. "What brings the likes of two landlubbers as you out into the middle of the sea?"

"We're lost at sea, good seagull, and we wonder if you can you help us return to Stanley Park where we live," replied Sammy.

"Stanley Park, you say," pondered the seagull. "Never heard of it. But if you can let me rest my tired wings and offer a bite to eat, I might be able to help you. They call me Salty, by the way, Salty Seagull."

Sammy and Rodney opened their packs and gave

Salty an acorn and a few clams, which he gladly gobbled up, then told them what he knew.

"The ocean current is carrying you along at a rapid speed, mates. It could be weeks, but you'll eventually reach land. Now, if this will lead to your Stanley Park or not, I can't say for sure."

"Weeks?" cried Rodney. "But we have no water and only a little food."

"Well," said Salty, "you've been kind to me, mates, so I've set my mind to do the same for you. I'll pass the word to my sea friends that you two landlubbers are adrift in your little boat and are in need of help. I'm sorry, but it's the best I can do."

"No need to be sorry. That would be a great help. Thank you!" said Sammy.

Rested and fed, Salty flew off. Sammy and Rodney watched until he once again became a tiny speck in the sky, then disappeared completely. Now they were alone again and wondered if Salty Seagull would keep his word to help them.

Time passed and the sun reached the horizon. The sky darkened and the air cooled. Sammy and Rodney shivered a bit from the cold night air of the sea. They put on their green and brown sweaters, which would not serve as good camouflage in a rowboat adrift at sea, but would keep them warm throughout the long night. And soon they fell asleep.

Sammy stirred for a moment, then began to dream of wild, fanciful things—that he was falling—down, down, down into the unlit abyss of the ocean. In the dark depths, he saw hundreds of strange and startling eyes—large ones, small ones, narrow ones, wide ones—all looking back at him. And, although he strained to get a better look, he couldn't make out the shapes of the mysterious animals they belonged to.

Rodney was also dreaming and dreamt that they had arrived at an island that had leafy green bushes with unusual fruits hanging from them. He reached out and took one that looked like a marshmallow, oddly enough, but was a dark purple colour. He sniffed it, and the marvellous scent of huckleberries poured over him.

Huckleberry marshmallows! he gleefully thought and put one in his mouth. But as soon as he did, the marshmallow disappeared. He took another, but it vanished, too. And so did all the others as he repeated this ritual again and again, and just when he was certain that he would be doomed to repeat this unsuccessfully forever…they both awoke with a start!

6

Odyssey, Poseidon and Neptune

Something—or someone—had jolted the boat with a great force. Rodney and Sammy, now fully alert, cautiously peered over the side. A shiny, smooth, bluish-gray lump flashed through the water. Then another similar lump appeared and yet another. Rodney and Sammy stared at the three peculiar shapes. Suddenly eyes appeared in one and then snouts above the water line. The strangest-looking sea animals, who seemed to have permanent smiles, gazed up at them.

"Are you friendly fish of some kind?" enquired Sammy hesitantly.

"We're dolphins!" came the reply by all three, and they made a clacking noise that appeared to be laughter. It was a pleasant sound, and their voices were cheery and childlike.

"Oh, I see," said Rodney, wondering if this was a new dream and hoping it would be more satisfying than the last one.

"We got word down south that you two were lost and needed help," said one of the dolphins.

"We normally don't swim this far north, but the situation sounded serious," added another.

"Are you all right?" asked the third dolphin.

"Well, considering everything, I suppose we're all right," said Sammy. "But we do need some help. We want to return to Stanley Park; it's where we live, you see, but we don't know which direction to row in to get there."

"There's no fresh water on board either," Rodney added anxiously.

As the dolphins looked at each other, their permanent smiles made the two little animals in the boat feel hopeful that things were going to work out.

"We don't know where your Stanley Park is, but there is land ahead, so it might help if we take you there," said the largest dolphin, who appeared to be the leader. "As for fresh water, the rain is sure to come. If you have something to hold rainwater in, we can guarantee you'll have enough to drink."

"Any help you can give us would be greatly appreciated, dear dolphins of the sea," said Rodney, still wondering if he had dreamt up such remarkable creatures.

"Follow us, then," said the leader, moving in front of the boat while the other dolphins positioned themselves one on either side.

Then Sammy took one oar and Rodney took the other, and they both started to row in unison, watching the wonderful dolphins as they swam. They seemed to dance in the water, leaping up now and again, but not the way the frogs in Stanley Park did—it was much more graceful than that. They were truly at home in the sea, and Sammy wondered if such strange animals as these would ever be able to climb a tree.

Silly squirrel, he thought. *Squirrels are meant for trees, and dolphins, quite clearly, are meant for oceans.*

In the meantime, Rodney was wondering how the dolphins cleaned their food, for they didn't seem to have any paws. *But then why would they need to clean their food,* he thought, *since it's already washed and salted for them right there in the ocean. What lucky animals!*

"Look there," said Sammy. "There's a cloud in the sky and a touch of rain is falling. Let's row to it."

"As fast as we can," Rodney responded.

Once under the cloud, they took out empty clam shells to catch the fresh rain water and drank. Refuelled and revitalized, they continued to row.

Day followed day followed day in exactly the same manner. At night the dolphins disappeared to rest beneath the surface of the ocean. And every morning they would reappear, smiling happily, ready to continue the journey when the two little animals awoke.

The dancing and leaping dolphins provided excellent entertainment for Sammy and Rodney and kept their spirits up—necessary considering the long, hard rowing they had to perform. And they helped break the boredom of looking at nothing but the ocean.

The rowing developed a rhythm after some time, and Rodney made up a little song that suited the rhythm quite nicely. It went like this:

Two little animals lost at sea
Two little animals, you and me
Rowing, rowing, where will we go?
Nobody's sure, but what do you know?
Along came the dolphins, kind and true
To help us get there through the blue
Ocean, ocean all around
All you can hear is the rowing sound.

Then one morning the expressions on the dolphins' faces changed. The permanent smiles were still there, but their eyes had a worried look.

"It will rain today," the dolphin leader said. "So you'll get more of the fresh water you need, but I warn you a storm is coming and the waves might rise very high. If the storm gets fierce, you should crouch down under the seat of the boat and hang on."

"During the storm, we must swim underwater," said another dolphin. "But don't be afraid—we'll be near you at all times."

At that very moment the sky darkened, and as a light rain started to fall, Sammy and Rodney took out their raincoats and put them on. Then they took out their teapot, removed the lid, and placed it so that they could catch all the fresh water that fell.

It rained lightly for some time and soon the teapot was filled. So they replaced the lid and bound the teapot tightly with strips of slippery seaweed the dolphins had tossed into the rowboat for them to use. Then they put the teapot into Sammy's pack and, using more seaweed, tied both packs onto the seat of the boat. Finally, they each took a long piece of thick seaweed and tied one end around their waists and the other end to the seat, as the dolphins had instructed.

"There must be quite a storm brewing if we have to tie ourselves down like this," Rodney said anxiously.

"Well, look what a storm can do in Stanley Park," replied Sammy. "It could get just as bad as that, and we have nowhere to run and hide out here on the ocean."

But it did not get just as bad as a storm in Stanley Park. It got worse. Much, much worse. It was like nothing Sammy or Rodney had ever seen, heard, or imagined before.

The rain thundered down in awful torrents into the boat and everywhere, and the wind screamed and howled in the most odious way. Rodney wanted to shout, "It's raining people and pets!" as the old animal saying went, but he didn't, because the old saying could not describe this stormy nightmare. There was no animal expression for it. It was like the sea had turned upside down and was now pouring on them from above.

The rowboat tossed every which way, and the two little animals hid under the seat as best they could, clinging to it for dear life. One minute they were carried by the waves up, up, up as high as a small mountain and the next minute, down, down, down, into a valley between wave crests.

"Will it ever end?" cried Sammy, his paws now cold and tired from all the exertion of hanging on. Just as he loosened his grip for an instant, the strip of seaweed holding him to the boat snapped, and all of a sudden he was gone!

"Sammy, Sammy, come back!" shouted Rodney as loud as he could. "Oh dear, oh no, oh dear!" he cried.

Sammy tossed in the water and turned in all sorts of directions. Then suddenly he felt himself propelled upwards and into the rainy air. The leader of the dolphins had swum under him! Now

he lifted Sammy out of the water on his snout and with one muscular flip and an extremely sharp eye, landed him right back in the boat!

Rodney grabbed Sammy by his coat collar and pulled him to safety under the seat again. As they felt a sudden movement beneath them, the two very wet, wide-eyed and frightened animals looked at each other—completely speechless. The little rowboat started to go in a direct line along the trough between two huge waves. It moved as if it had a motor, zooming along the wave's depression. There was no more tossing and turning, no more up, up, up or down, down, down. What was going on?

Then Sammy realized what it was. The three dolphins were directly under the boat, pushing it along with all their strength to get the two animals out of the storm.

"Hooray for dolphins!" he stood up and shouted. "Beautiful, wonderful, smiling, courageous dolphins!"

Rodney thought Sammy had really lost his nut this time and tried to force him to sit down. But by the time he succeeded in pushing him back down, the storm had passed on, and the boat had finally stopped. The three dolphins still smiled as they popped their heads out of the water, but now their eyes showed a deep fatigue.

"Thank you, dear dolphins. You've saved us from certain disaster," Sammy said, shedding tears of gratitude.

"We don't know how to thank you, dolphin friends. We truly don't," added Rodney. "And you know," he said, "through all of this, we've been so rude. We don't even know your names. We've been so busy thinking about ourselves."

Both the little animals felt terribly embarrassed at not having made proper introductions before this, and the dolphins were panting from exhaustion. But when they finally did get their voices back, they introduced themselves as Odyssey, Poseidon and Neptune. Rodney and Sammy had never heard of these unusual names before and found them very difficult to pronounce.

"Mind if we call you Odie, Posie and Neppy?" inquired Rodney rather sheepishly.

"Not a bit," said Neppy. "All our good friends call us that."

Night was falling, and everyone was tired from facing the terrible storm. So Odie, Posie and Neppy bid goodnight and slipped underneath the surface of the sea. The two little animal friends huddled together, and before either one could utter the "good" part of "goodnight" they were both sound asleep.

The three grinning dolphins had excited looks in their eyes the next morning.

"Good morning, you two!" Odie said in a happy voice. "We have some *very* good news. Look out at the horizon and tell us what you see."

Sammy and Rodney squinted their eyes and peered into the distance. A dark green mass appeared faintly ahead of them.

"Land!" they both shouted.

"Oh, I can't wait to get into the park!" Rodney said ecstatically.

"We must leave you, now that you are approaching land," Odie said sadly. "As we are citizens of the ocean, we cannot go any closer to land than this."

"Thank you, thank you, thank you!" said Rodney.

"Thank you a thousand times for your help!" added Sammy. "You've saved our lives. We will never forget your kindness to us."

Odyssey, Poseidon and Neptune bid adieu,

wished their animal friends good luck, and, as Sammy and Rodney began to row with renewed vigour, disappeared into the sea. Gradually the land mass ahead of them became larger, and the two little animals felt the excitement and anticipation of walking on hard ground once again amid the familiar sights of home.

7

Welcome to Nihon

'It doesn't look like Stanley Park at all," Sammy said as they approached land.

"No, it doesn't," replied Rodney in a discouraging tone. "There's no big sandy beach, and there are no tall trees or large bushes."

"Yes, the trees here are quite slim, and there are lots of small shrubs," Sammy added as he rowed toward the land. "I've never seen anything quite like it."

They headed for a little cove with a small rocky area where they could safely land. Then, just as they nestled into shore, Rodney jumped out and secured the boat.

"Where in the world do you think we are?" whispered Rodney, making sure that no one behind the dense foliage could hear him.

"Your guess is as good as mine," replied Sammy in the same hushed manner. "Let's have a look around."

They decided to follow a trail they spotted that led into the green hills. It was a narrow, winding trail, and the forest foliage was so thick they couldn't see anything beyond what was right in front of them. Finally, a clearing emerged at the end of which were two wide trails that went in opposite directions. Uncertain about which path to take, they performed "Rock, Paper, Scissors" with their paws.

"I win," Rodney said, "and I say we go that way," pointing to the trail on the left. And that way they went.

Now they were in flat terrain, and the trail was wide enough to allow them to walk side by side. Their curiosity mixed with fear as they examined the newly found greenery around them. Some of the trees had familiar shapes and leaves, but everything was on a smaller scale. There were maple trees all right, but the leaves were tiny compared to the fat leaves on the maple trees in Stanley Park.

Every now and again they passed a grove of several tall, narrow trees closely packed together.

They were an exquisite light green, and their slim branches overflowed with delicate, long leaves. Sammy thought they looked familiar, but couldn't recall where he'd seen them before. Then, all of a sudden, he remembered.

"Rodney, these are bamboo trees! I've read about them in *The Squirrel's Guide to Trees of the World*—only I just can't remember where the book said they were from."

"Japan!" said Rodney. "I think we're in Japan. I've read about bamboo trees, too, and I know they grow in Japan."

"Yes, you must be right!" agreed Sammy. "Can you believe this? I never, ever thought I'd see Japan!"

"You wanted to go beyond the outskirts of the park, didn't you?" sighed Rodney, sounding a bit dazed by it all. "Well, you certainly got your wish!"

"I wonder where all the animals are. There's no sign of any squirrels or raccoons, not even a bird," said Sammy.

"There might not be squirrels, raccoons *or* birds," Rodney replied nervously, "but think about those odd-looking dolphins we met. There might be strange-looking creatures here too. Dangerous ones, even."

"Maybe, but don't forget how generous and helpful the dolphins were."

"Yes, but will the animals in Japan be the same? Remember, there are good and bad animals everywhere; so we have to be cautious."

As the evening sun began to set, little birds appeared in the trees and sang a goodnight song to the sun as it slowly slipped from view. Feeling a bit tired, Sammy and Rodney found a tree stump to sit on. They took out the last remaining acorns and clams from their backpacks and started to eat, mindful that from now on they would have to find food in this new land.

Suddenly, Rodney heard a rustling and shuffling behind him. Unable to speak, the terrified raccoon elbowed his friend rather hard.

"Ouch...what did you do that for?" cried Sammy angrily.

Rodney, whose eyes were now large and saucer-like with fear, made a slight gesture with his head to indicate something was behind them. Sammy's eyes locked onto his friend's, and he immediately stopped eating and listened. Now he could hear what Rodney had heard—a rustling in the bushes and a shuffling on the ground.

"We'd better turn around and look," whispered Sammy, "or we might be devoured by an enormous Japanese...who-knows-what!"

So the two friends counted "one, two, three" and turned, expecting to see the who-knows-what waiting with its teeth bared and mouth open. But standing about ten feet away was a slim young deer with large, curious eyes.

Sammy and Rodney looked at each other and sighed in relief. There were deer who lived in Stanley Park, and although a bit stand-offish, they were generally known to be kind animals.

"Japanese deer can't be so different from their cousins across the sea," Sammy murmured to Rodney.

"Hello!" said Rodney in the

friendliest tone he could muster. "My name is Rodney Raccoon, and this is my good friend, Sammy Squirrel. And you are...?"

The deer bowed its head in a greeting and then looked up at them. "My name is Shika," she said in a soft, gentle voice. "I have never seen animals like you before. Do you live near here?"

"No," replied Sammy. "We're from across the ocean. We live in Stanley Park. You've probably never heard of it, but you might know of Canada. That's what the people call it, anyway."

"Oh, you are from Canada. Yes, I have indeed heard of it. How wonderful!" she gushed and bowed her head again. "Welcome to Nihon! That's what we call our country in our language. You probably know it as Japan. I hear the deer in

Canada live in immense, ancient forests where there is delicious grass and water in an endless supply. You are so lucky to be from there."

"There is a lot of land and water, I suppose, but we live in a park, as I told you. We don't know too much about what's outside of it," Rodney answered. This new acquaintance was certainly more polite and generous with her praise than any deer he had met in Stanley Park. The way she kept bowing her head was so gentle and graceful that Rodney wanted to bow right back, but it felt a little funny, so he didn't.

"I live in a park, too!" Shika said.

"Are there large trees in your park...and greenery? Is it quite green with bushes and shrubs... and ferns?" asked Sammy, feeling homesick now.

"What about berries? Are there huckleberries or blackberries? Is there a lake or a lagoon?" asked Rodney.

"Would you like to see for yourself?" Shika offered, unable to answer so many rapid-fire questions.

"Oh, yes!" the two animals shouted together.

"We would like to see your park and rest a bit there before we return to our own," replied

Rodney, secretly wondering to himself how and if they would ever get back home.

"Hop on my back then, and we'll leave right away," said Shika.

So the two little animals from Canada jumped onto Shika's back. The young deer leaped into the woods and took them on a journey through the Japanese forests. They passed through gorgeous green groves of majestic bamboo, climbed up hills and trotted around corners into lush foliage and woods filled with maple trees in full autumn bloom and intoxicatingly beautiful. Rich reds, yellows and browns dazzled the visitors. Escorted by Shika, their guide, they plunged into little valleys with narrow streams and passed enchanting waterfalls with placid ponds.

It soon became clear that the world beyond Stanley Park was indeed a beautiful place and that this adventure was the best thing Sammy and Rodney had ever done together. And, for a moment at least, the trials and tribulations of their journey across the sea were all but forgotten.

8

The Kindness of Strangers

As the sun set, the threesome left the forest and entered the outskirts of a city. They had travelled for almost a full day now and were feeling very tired.

"We'll soon be in Nara," Shika said. "I think you'll like it. It's an ancient city with an enormous park."

Turning a corner, they came upon a large grassy meadow filled with hundreds of deer—some of them resting, others strolling, and many little ones happily playing. Sammy and Rodney had never seen so many deer in one place before.

"Welcome, Sammy-san and Rodney-san," said Shika warmly, using the Japanese suffix indicating respect. "Welcome to Nara Park."

The two little animals jumped from Shika's

back and stepped onto the grassy meadow. After so many hours climbing hills and travelling through dense forests, the open meadow with its soft green carpet made them all feel immediately at home.

Several deer came up to them, bowed their heads, and looked at them curiously.

"Welcome home, Shika-san," said one of the deer. "You must be tired from your journey. Who are your two little friends?"

Shika introduced Sammy and Rodney, and all the deer were quite excited to meet foreign animals for the first time.

"How many deer live in Nara Park?" asked Sammy.

"Over a thousand deer live here," Shika said. "Our ancestors were invited here by the Japanese people many years ago, and it has become our home."

"Did you say they invited you?" asked Sammy. "Invited you to live here?"

"Well, our ancestors came here and were welcomed and allowed to remain."

"To be invited by people to live in a beautiful park is a very kind thing. They must be like our Lord Stanley," said Rodney to his friend. "You see, Sammy, not all people are unkind to animals. I knew it, I just knew it."

"But what about pets?" inquired Sammy. "Don't people and pets come into the park and run at the animals to scare them?"

"Very few people bring their pets here," replied one of the other deer. "Anyway, if pets come along, they are very small and ignore us. Perhaps we scare them by our size."

"Actually, the people here are very kind to us," added another deer. "They often give us delicious grain biscuits made especially for the park animals."

"They bow to us in greeting when they give us the biscuits, and we bow our heads back in thanks. Everyone is quite polite here in Nara Park," added Shika.

Sammy and Rodney were surprised to hear this and wanted to know more about the animals and the people in Nara Park.

"How can you get along so well and be so polite to each other?" asked Sammy.

"Japan is a very small country with a large population," Shika explained. "So harmony within the group is very important if we are all to get along. That goes for both the people and the animals here. Actually, it's easy for us because from a young age we're taught the importance of respect and getting along."

"Maybe that's our problem back home in Stanley Park," mused Sammy. "We are too busy thinking about our individual selves, and that causes problems."

Sammy and Rodney asked more questions about life in Nara Park, and the deer asked many questions in return about life in Stanley Park. Finally, the weary travellers became sleepy and found a spot near some trees at the edge of the meadow, where they drifted off into a delicious sleep.

There were many dreams that evening. Some of the deer dreamt of a far-off park with unusual animals and towering trees surrounded by a vast sea. The squirrel dreamt of bowing animals, people and lush bamboo groves, while the raccoon dreamt of tasty, grainy biscuits and friendly people walking with their pets.

In the morning, the deer invited Sammy and Rodney to join them in a breakfast of the tasty,

thin, round biscuits Shika had told them about.
There was a small stream nearby, so Sammy made
green leaf tea to wash down the meal. He offered
it to Shika and a few of her friends, and the deer
kept repeating an odd-sounding word as they sipped
the tea.

"*Oishi, oishi.*"

"What is this word that everyone keeps
saying?" asked Sammy.

"Delicious, it's delicious!" replied Shika. "They
like your green leaf tea very much." Most of the
deer knew a bit of English, all having attended
Fawn School, but it was Shika who knew the
most.

After completing their hearty, international
breakfast, Shika, Sammy and Rodney decided to
take a walk through the park. They passed by a
stream that meandered through a woodsy area
where birds sang morning songs, and the stream
gurgled a bubbly greeting to all.

"It seems like such a friendly place," said Rodney.

"It does, indeed," replied Sammy.

They crossed a red bridge that arched over the
stream and entered a long, wide gravel path lined
on both sides with hundreds of stone lanterns.

In the distance, they saw a strange-looking tall wooden structure composed of five tiers. The bottom tier was the largest and each tier above was a little smaller than the one below.

"What kind of a place is that, Shika-san?" asked Rodney, adding the "san" onto Shika's name as he had heard all the deer do when they spoke.

"It's a pagoda," said Shika matter-of-factly. "Pagodas are built by Japanese people. Some people like to come and admire them and some come to meditate. It relaxes them, I suppose."

Rodney and Sammy had never seen people meditating in Stanley Park, although they had often seen people silently stare at the park totem poles. Perhaps those people, like the Japanese, were doing a kind of meditation.

Walking farther along the path, they passed an enclosure with a very tall fence around it. Shika stopped for a moment, looked at the fence and shivered slightly.

"Let's move along. I don't like this part of the park," she said.

"What's that fenced-in area for?" asked Sammy, curious about Shika's sudden discomfort.

"That," she said in a low, sad voice, "is where the deer antler-removing ceremony is held. Once a year the caretakers herd the male deer into that fenced area and remove their antlers. It is a very frightening experience for the males, one which makes them feel ashamed and defenceless."

"That's a cruel thing to do," said Sammy.

"Why would the caretakers do such a thing, Shika-san?" Rodney asked. "I thought you said people are kind to animals here."

"There are many visitors to Nara Park, and the caretakers are afraid that the antlers of our male deer might harm someone. But we would never harm any visitors here, and that's something the caretakers just don't understand."

The three animals silently walked down the path and thought about the injustice of that.

"No matter where you live, misunderstandings seem bound to occur," said Sammy.

The day passed quickly as the three animals wandered through Nara Park. They chatted amiably and compared the differences between their homelands. Their tour complete, Sammy and Rodney hopped onto Shika's back and returned to the meadow where they had seen all the deer gathered the day before.

"There's something odd here," said Sammy, as the deer came into view. "I can't quite put my paw on it, but something seems to be missing."

As they entered the meadow, several deer rushed up to Shika and spoke all at once, so that no one could make sense of what they said.

"Please, everyone, don't jabber. What's the matter?" asked Shika.

"The caretakers were here," said one of the deer anxiously. "They came this afternoon while you were gone and took most of the male deer with them."

"They're going to hold the antler-removing ceremony tomorrow, and there's nothing we can do about it," added an elderly female deer.

Sammy felt a sudden sadness in his heart. "Now I know why the view of the park seemed so odd when we first got back. There's not one antler in sight!"

"There must be something we can do to help our new friends," Rodney said with concern.

"They've been so kind and generous to us," Sammy added. But Rodney couldn't think of a thing.

Then suddenly Sammy got an idea and excitedly whispered it to Rodney and Shika. And though the deer nearby couldn't hear what Sammy said, they could definitely hear what the other two were saying.

"Oh, my, my, my!" Shika replied.

"Could be dangerous!" added Rodney.

All the deer were extremely curious when Sammy finished talking and Shika finally broke the silence.

"Let's do it!" she said in a very determined tone. "We'll wait until dark and make our move." Then the three friends called the other deer over, and Sammy's animated whispering resumed once again as he explained his daring plan.

When darkness fell and the time had come to make their move, Shika, Sammy and Rodney bowed to the other deer and headed for the trail that led across the stream and over the red bridge. It was this very path that would take them to the fenced enclosure where the male deer now awaited their fate the following day.

As they approached the outskirts of the meadow, they turned and looked back at their companions.

"Ganbatte!" shouted one of the deer.

"That means 'Do your best!'" Shika said. "It's used when someone is about to face great difficulty."

The three animals proceeded down the trail and quickly disappeared from view. As they moved through the dark and crossed the red bridge, they entered the wide, long, gravel path. It was a special Japanese festival day; each one of the hundreds of stone lanterns along the path had a lit candle placed inside that guided the three brave friends through the long, dark night. Finally, they arrived at their destination, turned off the path, and stopped in front of the fenced enclosure for deer.

Shika stood directly beside the fence as Sammy and Rodney jumped onto her back. Now that they could reach the top, they easily climbed over it and into the enclosure below where hundreds of deer stood looking at them, wide-eyed in surprise.

"Don't be alarmed," whispered Rodney, "We're here to help you escape."

"Show us where the gate is," said Sammy.

One of the deer pointed his antlers at the far end of the fence, where a gate was held shut with a long piece of wood. It only needed to be pushed out of the latch for the gate to open, but the two little animals would need to stand on the back of one of the imprisoned deer to push the long wooden bar aside.

"One of you come over here quickly, so we can stand on your back," requested Sammy.

And as a young buck stepped toward them, the two little animals jumped onto his back. Then Sammy and Rodney started to push the long piece of wood with their paws. It moved easily out of the latch and within seconds the gate was open.

"Now all of you, go quietly out of the gate and head for the meadow!" whispered Sammy.

Everyone moved quickly through the gate, and with Shika leading the way, the deer silently headed through the dark woods toward their home meadow. But just as Sammy and Rodney pushed the gate shut, they heard a loud voice.

A caretaker was shouting angrily and waving his arms. He started to run toward Sammy, Rodney and the young buck.

"Let's get out of here!" said Sammy.

The two little animals hung on tightly as the young buck leaped into action with the caretaker

in pursuit. The buck headed down a narrow path at the back of the enclosure, where the branches made an arched canopy so that not even the moonlight could get through.

He ran faster than he had ever run before, turned a corner along the way, and jumped into the thick woods by the edge of the path. The three animals, hidden by the dense vegetation there, watched as the caretaker ran past and off into the distance.

"He's gone," the young buck said. "That path leads to a temple outside the park; so we won't be seeing him for some time." Then they turned and quickly moved through the woods to rejoin the other deer. When they had all arrived at the meadow, the deer broke into joyous cheers.

"Hurray for our friends, Sammy-san and Rodney-san. Hurray for Shika-san!"

That night there was dancing and prancing in the meadow as the deer celebrated their great escape.

"But what will happen now?" Rodney asked. "Will the caretakers come for the deer again and try to herd them back to that horrible place?"

"The male deer will go into the hills on the

outskirts of the park," replied Shika, "to hide for a few days until things quiet down."

The following day, Rodney and Sammy saw signs posted all over the park saying the antler-removing ceremony had been cancelled, so the deer seemed safe for now.

But as the two friends rested quietly in the meadow with the female deer and their fawns, Rodney suddenly wondered, "Do you think it's time for us to leave, Sammy? It's beautiful here, but I miss Stanley Park and our friends."

"I miss the tall trees and our dear friends, too. But how are we going to get back?" worried Sammy.

"You have helped us greatly," said Shika, "and now we want to help you. Tomorrow morning I will take you back to your boat. We have gathered enough grain biscuits to last your whole trip and will also give you fresh water to take. There are many water containers in the park for us, so you can take one with you."

"Wonderful!" exclaimed Rodney and Sammy simultaneously.

And so it was decided that four deer would accompany them back to the boat. One would bring the biscuits while two others would take turns transporting the water container, and Shika would again carry the two little friends on her back. Everyone quickly moved into action; supplies were gathered and then the oldest female deer stepped forward to address them.

"We, the deer of Nara Park, want to humbly thank you for your help in freeing our fellow deer. We will never forget what you have done for us. May your journey be filled with ease and the joy of knowing you are going home," she said, and then bowed deeply to Sammy and Rodney.

Without a word, and in complete unison, hundreds of deer turned and bowed deeply to Sammy and Rodney. The two little animals bowed deeply back.

"We also thank you for your kindness in welcoming without reservation two strangers from a faraway land," said Sammy.

"I'm not as good with words as my friend," said Rodney, "but I want to say something, too. I will never forget you. You were wonderful to us, and your biscuits are scrumptious."

Everyone chuckled at Rodney's words of thanks. But before anyone could get teary-eyed, the four deer and the two little Canadians set off for the Japanese coast. The sight of hundreds of deer bowing in a heartfelt goodbye would be forever etched in the hearts of Sammy and Rodney.

They moved on in silence, each one deep in thought, reflecting on how these recent friendships had altered their worlds. It was no longer possible for either the deer or Sammy and Rodney to think of animals from other places as strangers. The bond could not be broken or forgotten.

After a full day of travel, the hills near the coast came into view. Up and down through the winding path went the six animals until they came to the small rocky cove where the boat was stowed. They loaded the supplies on board, and then it was time to say a final goodbye.

"We'll miss you, Sammy-san and Rodney-san," said Shika sadly. "Please don't ever forget us."

"We'll never forget you, Shika-san," said Sammy, feeling a lump in his throat and suddenly strangely lost for words.

"Never," added Rodney, who knew that nothing more needed to be said.

As Sammy and Rodney got into the boat,

the four deer on the rocky beach bowed deeply, looked up, then bowed again.

"Ganbatte!" they shouted. "Sayonara, Sammy-san and Rodney-san!"

The deer began heading toward the woods, but turned for one long, last look, as Sammy and Rodney rowed away from the shore.

9

Winifred Whale

Sammy and Rodney rowed silently for hours, both experiencing a mix of emotions.

I hope we don't encounter another terrible storm, Rodney worried to himself.

I hope the dolphins and the seagull will help us again, Sammy kept wishing.

Otherwise, who knows where we'll end up, the two of them thought simultaneously.

But there was no storm on the horizon and no sign of the seagull or the three smiling dolphins. It was a sunny day and the waves were calm as the islands of Japan disappeared from their view. Rodney, feeling tired and a bit discouraged, was the first one to break their silence.

"Let's take a rowing break and have a snack."

"Sounds like an excellent idea."

So they took out some grain biscuits from their packs and that was when Rodney noticed what looked like a small, barren island in the distance.

"Do you see that island up ahead?" Rodney asked.

"Yes, I do," said Sammy, squinting a bit to get a better look.

"Maybe we should go and rest there for a while," Rodney suggested. "A sea bird might pass by and we could ask for some help."

"Another excellent idea!" said Sammy.

So they took up their oars again and started toward the barren island.

"That's odd," said Rodney. "The island is completely gray. Not a bit of green on it."

"Maybe it's an island made of rock," said Sammy.

Suddenly a fountain of water from the island shot into the air and came back down again.

"It has a fountain," said Rodney. "Isn't that strange."

"Not only that, but the island is moving," said Sammy. "I swear it is!"

"What a curious place," mused Rodney.

"L-L-Look," stuttered Sammy. "The island...or

whatever it is…has an eye! And it just blinked at us. It isn't an island! It's alive!"

"I've seen a lot of things at sea before but never two little animals the likes of you!" the sea creature said in a booming voice. "What are you?"

"My name is Sammy Squirrel and this is my friend, Rodney Raccoon. We're park animals, actually, and we're lost at sea. Do you think you can help us get home?"

The large sea creature studied them.

"I've come across people lost at sea before and have helped them get home; so I suppose I could do the same for you. My name is Winifred, Winifred Whale, that is. Where do you want to go?" she asked.

"We're heading for Stanley Park in Canada. Would you happen to know the way?" asked Rodney meekly, feeling unnerved by Winifred's size and tremendous voice.

"Speak up a bit, will you!" she boomed. "Your voice is as soft as your size is small. Where is it you want to go?"

"To Stanley Park, our home in Canada," Rodney said, this time loud enough for Winifred to hear.

"I've never heard of Stanley Park, but I certainly know where Canada is. I spend a large part of the year living off the Canadian coast. I know the way quite well. It's not the usual season for me to go there, but I can make a detour and pass by."

"Thank you, Winifred, that would be most kind," said Sammy.

"I'll be back in a minute," said Winifred, as she dropped below the surface. Moments later, large waves splashed around the little rowboat as she resurfaced with a thick cord of seaweed in her mouth.

"Here, tie this to your boat," she said. And they did so, quite in awe of the massive whale right beside them. "I'll hold the other end and pull you along. Much faster than rowing, I can guarantee you that," Winifred chuckled. "Now hold on tight, little park animals!"

As Winifred moved away from the boat, the waves she made rocked it up and down. But when she was some distance away, the boat started to glide through the water. Gradually, she increased her speed and the rowboat skipped over the waves.

"Whee!" said Rodney.

"Whoopee!" said Sammy.

The boat zoomed along and bounced over the waves, providing a thrilling cruise at great speed.

"Hang on!" said Winifred as she plowed through a large wave.

Sammy and Rodney rose a foot into the air, plopped back down again, and broke into giggles.

"Faster, Winifred, faster!" Sammy delightedly screamed.

The days passed by quickly, and the sea storms were never a problem. Whenever Winifred saw one off in the distance, she just made a large detour around it. And in the evenings, the three animals stopped and swapped stories about life in Stanley Park, adventures in Japan, and about the mysterious world under the sea.

"Are there berries under the sea?" Rodney inquired one evening.

"And are there underwater trees?" asked Sammy.

Winifred laughed, causing a big wave to rock the rowboat back and forth.

"Are there beautiful coral reefs in Stanley Park?" asked Winifred. "And are there lots of places to swim there?"

"No reefs that I know of," said Sammy. "And certainly nowhere in the park to swim for someone your size. But you could swim in English Bay all you like."

"I would like to visit your world under the sea," said Rodney. But he knew that being on top of it was the closest he would ever get.

"And I would like to visit your world, too, but it does seem impossible," observed Winifred. "Maybe some things are better left to the imagination."

10

Oh, Stanley Park!

Time passed quickly for the happy little group of sea travellers, until early one morning, Sammy spotted what looked like a thin green line along the distant horizon.

"Look over there, Rodney," Sammy said.

"Over where? There's nothing to look at except sea and more sea everywhere. "

"I mean that thin green line on the horizon. Do you think that's home...that it's Stanley Park?"

"That's the coast of Canada, my friends," Winifred said. "Though I've never been close enough to tell if there's a park there."

At once the two little animals felt a deep and heartfelt longing for home, and a familiar tune started to sound inside Sammy's head.

Ta TA ta-ta...Ta TA ta-ta it went, over and

over again, until at last Sammy felt compelled to sing it out loud.

"Ta TA ta-ta...Ta TA ta-ta..." he cried out.

"I know what song that is!" Rodney said breaking into a big grin. "We learned it at the Park School for Animals."

"But I can't remember how it goes," said Sammy. The words were on the tip of his tongue, but they were unwilling to make the leap out of his mouth.

"Oh, Stanley Park!" sang Rodney Raccoon proudly. "Oh, Stanley Park!"

"Now I remember," said Sammy. "Let's sing!"

And with a "one, two, three, four" they sang out:

Oh, Stanley Park
Our home and favourite land
Big Douglas firs
Where owls hoot, oh so grand
With cedar trees
And surrounding seas
You can walk there all you like
There's a little lake
Where the beavers make
The best dams in the world

Oh, Stanley Park
The animals live free
Oh, Stanley Park
Was made for you and me
Oh, Stanley Park
Was made for you—and—me.

"What a wonderful song!" said Winifred as the two little animals sat silently thinking of their home and friends who were only a short distance away. Winifred loved the sea with all her heart, so she understood what this beautiful song meant to the two little animals she had found so far away from their home.

"I can't take you any closer now or I might get stuck in shallow water; so you'll have to row the rest of the way on your own. But I've enjoyed our time together very much, dear little Rodney and Sammy."

"And so have we!" Sammy said. "Thank you for your kindness, Winifred."

"I wish there was something we could do for you," added Rodney.

"Well...if you ever see a whale beached on the shore, you must try to help that whale somehow. That is what you can do for me."

"We promise," Sammy said solemnly. "Goodbye, Winifred!"

"Goodbye, and safe journey!" said Rodney.

Winifred turned, waved her tail at them and was gone deep into the ocean, leaving Sammy and Rodney alone again. But Stanley Park was now in sight, and they rowed toward it with all their might. First the tall trees of the park came into view, and then they could see the sandy beaches. Next came the outline of the seawall around the park, and people walking along with their pets.

"Oh, even the sight of people and pets on the seawall makes me happy," said Sammy.

"Stanley Park is only minutes away!" added Rodney.

11

Home Sweet Home

"Over there," said Sammy as they approached Stanley Park. "There's a secluded part of the beach that looks like a good place to bring the boat in."

As they neared shore, they stopped rowing and let the gentle waves lift the bow of the boat onto the sand, and then they jumped out.

They were a little wobbly because of so many days spent at sea, but they regained their balance enough to dash across the sand. Their only obstacle was the seawall path that lay directly ahead of them. Beyond that was a small arch in the bushes which would take them deep into the forest. But after leaping up onto the seawall they suddenly stopped. Sitting on a bench next to the bush archway was a man, a

woman, a little boy and a dog.

"Look at that!" said the boy excitedly. "A squirrel and a raccoon!"

The three people looked at Sammy and Rodney, and Sammy and Rodney looked back at them as the dog sat up and opened its eyes wide.

"We don't want to scare them," the man said. "So let's just sit here and watch them."

"I think they want to go into the bushes; so we should be quiet and leave them alone. This is their home, after all," the woman added.

The dog's tail began to wag, and the three people remained seated with soft smiles on their faces.

"I don't know if we should go into the park this way," whispered Sammy. "Those people are a bit too close to the forest arch for my liking. What if they jump up and start chasing us?"

"They look pretty friendly," Rodney whispered back. "And remember what Shika said about how kind people can be. People and animals can get along if they respect each other. Let's just bow the way the deer in Nara Park do. And then we can be on our way."

"Good idea, Rodney," said Sammy.

Rodney and Sammy stepped forward, then bowed their heads slightly and dashed across the seawall path. They quickly slipped under the arch and into the woods of the park.

"There, you see," said Rodney. "They were as friendly as could be."

But Sammy wasn't listening. He looked up and around at the soaring trees, the dew-laden ferns, the thick bushes and the silky moss. Seeing all the glorious greenery made him tremble with excitement. He knew every tree, every twist and every turn in the trail. Someone could have blindfolded him, and he still would have found his way home with ease.

As they walked deep into the park, the majestic fir tree where Sammy lived slowly came into view. They could see the windows of Sammy's house high above the lower tree branches.

"Home, home, sweet, sweet home!" sighed Sammy, who quickly darted up the tree and then threw down the rope ladder to his friend.

"It all seems like a dream, doesn't it?" asked Rodney a little while later as they sat in armchairs and sipped green leaf tea in front of the fireplace.

"A strange, wonderful dream indeed," Sammy agreed, "except for these." And he passed Rodney a grain biscuit that Shika-san had given them.

12

The End is the Beginning

The years passed by, but Sammy Squirrel and Rodney Raccoon never forgot their adventure beyond the outskirts of Stanley Park. Every Sunday they walked over to the cliff edge to look out at the Great Ocean. Some days they thought they could see a barren island moving slowly on the horizon. And near the island were three distant figures jumping in and out of the water.

Was it Winifred the Whale and the three dolphins, Odie, Posie and Neppy passing by to say hello? the two friends often wondered.

Once a month, Sammy and Rodney gave a talk at Old Hollow Hall about their adventures beyond the outskirts of Stanley Park. The younger animals always had a multitude of questions about the people and animals who lived outside the park and in and beyond the sea.

"What are the people like?"

"Are they kind?"

"What about the animals? Are they dangerous?" they asked.

The questions went on and on, and Sammy and Rodney answered all of them patiently until they were tired. Then they ended their talk by reminding everyone of the common bond they shared with all living things.

"Underneath it all, people and animals are the same everywhere," Rodney said. "Some treat you kindly and some do not."

"Be careful, of course," added Sammy. "But always be kind and respectful to others, when you begin your own adventures."

"And may you always find friends, wherever you go," Rodney smiled.

Duane Lawrence was born in Princeton, B.C. and now lives in Vancouver, B.C., where he teaches high school French and enjoys regular walks in beautiful Stanley Park. It was during one leisurely stroll in the park that he decided to write about the animals that live there. Duane also taught English in central Japan for nine years and was a high school French teacher in London, England for one year. Besides English, Duane speaks French and Japanese.